The Adventures of
Titch & Mitch

The Adventures of
Titch & Mitch

Book 2
The Trolls of Sugar Loaf Wood

Garth Edwards
Illustrated by Max Stasyuk

INSIDE POCKET

Published in Great Britain by Inside Pocket Publishing Limited

First published in Great Britain in 2010

Text © Garth Edwards, 2009

Illustrations © Inside Pocket Publishing Limited

Titch and Mitch is a registered trade mark of Inside Pocket Publishing
Limited

A CIP catalogue record for this book is available from the British Library

ISBN 978-0-9562315-1-2

Inside Pocket Publishing Limited Reg. No. 06580097

Printed and bounds in Great Britain by CPI Bookmarque Ltd, Croydon

www.insidepocket.co.uk

For N & J

Contents

Map of Island

Dragon Mouse Cave

Magic Valley

Cedric's Cave

Wendy's House

Lake

Wiffen's and Perry's Cottage

Sugar Bread Mines

Turkey Farm

1

The End of the Rainbow

TITCH AND MITCH WERE TWO PIXIE
brothers who just loved to have parties. They lived
on a small island not far off the coast, and one fine
day they arranged to have a garden party. Friends
from all over the island joined them and soon they
were all tucking in to a lovely meal of fresh bread,
fruits and wild mushrooms.

Shortly after lunch, a shadow passed over them.
Titch looked up and saw black clouds tumbling in
from over the sea. "It looks like rain is on the way,"
he said with disappointment. Titch was a little bit
taller than his brother, nearly as tall as a squirrel. He
had thick curly hair, blue eyes and was always full of

energy.

Mitch was a year younger, with a cheerful smiling face and always wore a green woolly hat. He too looked anxiously at the sky and as he did a great big drop of water splashed on to his nose.

A few moments later the rain started to fall. Luckily, most of the guests had finished eating, and the rain didn't bother Willy Water Rat and the Beaver family because they liked water anyway. But Titch and Mitch, Budgie the seagull and their rabbit friends scuttled indoors and peeped out of the windows.

It was just a brief shower but as soon as it finished there appeared a magnificent rainbow, which started high in the sky and stretched over the sea and finished in the

hills on the mainland. It was Old Bill the rabbit who announced that there was a great hoard of treasure to be found at the end of a rainbow.

"It's a well known fact," he said in a rather pompous way, "but nobody that I know has ever found it."

"I heard it was a pot of gold," agreed Budgie, "but

I've never looked for it."

"If there is treasure at the end of this particular rainbow," said Titch, "which is the biggest and best rainbow I have ever seen, then the treasure is probably the biggest and the best ever as well." Titch's eyes were bright as he stared at the beautiful colours sparkling in the sky.

"I know," said Mitch in a very excited voice, "let's jump on the magic bicycle and follow the rainbow while it is still bright. We can collect the treasure, bring it back to the island, and share it with all our friends."

Their friends thought this was a very good idea, so they clapped their hands and cheered, "Hurray for Titch and Mitch! We'll all be rich if you find the treasure, but you must be quick and go now before the rainbow disappears."

The sun was shining again, so Titch and Mitch tumbled all over each other in their hurry to climb on to the magic bicycle and follow the rainbow before it disappeared. With all their friends standing round them in the garden they called out the magic words, "Up, up and away!" The bicycle rose into the air and with Titch steering as usual, the two brothers set their sights on the far end of the rainbow, and headed off over the sea.

When they got near to the hills on the mainland, they saw that the rainbow actually

finished in a lake a bit further on. When they arrived at the lake, they found it now finished in a wood a bit more further on. When they reached the wood, they found the rainbow actually

finished high in some more hills a bit further on still.

"We'll never catch it," wailed Mitch.

"One more try," replied Titch pedalling with even greater determination.

This time the end of the rainbow appeared to be in a waterfall high in the hills and as they got near, it did not move further away, but stayed in the waterfall. The different colours of the rainbow sparkled in the water spray as they approached, so they landed on a nearby hill, marvelled at the colours and wondered where the treasure would be.

"I wonder if it's in the middle of the waterfall," said Mitch, trying to peer over the edge and look through the rushing water.

"I don't mind getting wet for a bit of treasure, but

all that water cascading down seems very dangerous," said Titch. He looked very doubtful as he frowned at the billowing clouds of spray.

Just then, they saw a little old man with skinny legs, bare feet and long hair running along a path towards the waterfall. All he wore was a loincloth made of an old sack and he hopped a lot as he scampered along. Reaching the waterfall, he simply disappeared behind the falling water.

"There must be a cave behind the waterfall!" exclaimed Mitch excitedly. "Come on Titch, let's follow him."

The pixies left

their bicycle and, climbing down the hillside as fast as they could, followed the path taken by the old man. They approached the waterfall and the spray of the water made them wetter and wetter the nearer they got to it. As it was very slippery and they were very frightened of falling in, they got down on their hands and knees and crawled along the path and into the waterfall.

Very soon, they found themselves crawling along a secret passageway.

"Look there," said Mitch pointing up ahead. In front of them, they could see a bright light. Heading towards it, they realised that the cave ceiling was high enough for them to stand up. The bright light led them into a vast cavern and they blinked as they

walked into it and looked around. The old man they had followed had his back to them and was sitting at a table in the middle of the cave. It was obviously his home because they saw a bed, a kitchen sink, a table, some chairs, a big cupboard and another table in an alcove.

Titch cleared his throat. "Hello," he said.

The man didn't move.

Thinking he might be a little deaf, Mitch shouted out loudly, "HELLO THERE."

Leaping high into the air, the little old man turned round and saw the two pixies. "Oh my goodness, you gave me such a turn. There's no need to shout. I'm not deaf, you know."

"Sorry," said Mitch.

"We sort of followed you through the waterfall," Titch added, lamely.

"Why?"

"We're looking for the end of the rainbow and we followed it all the way to the waterfall."

"Really?" said the old man. He had a wrinkled face, a long, straggly beard, blue eyes and was very thin. "Have you been following the rainbow for a long time?"

"Oh yes," said

Titch. "For ages. It kept moving further and further away, until finally it stopped right here at the waterfall."

"Ah, I see."

The old man nodded and looked at them quizzically. "And may I ask you, what are your names?

I've never met pixies before. You are pixies, I presume?"

"Yes, we are," Titch said proudly. "And very nice pixies we are too. My name is Titch and my brother here is called Mitch."

"My name is Cedric and I am a hermit. This is my cave and I live here all on my own."

"Don't you ever get lonely?" asked Mitch curiously.

"No, of course not. I just like to be on my own, so nobody disturbs me when I'm learning things."

"What are you learning?" asked Titch.

"Everything. Hermits are very wise people you know," replied Cedric. "Why don't you pixies come and sit down, have a cup of tea and tell me why you are following a rainbow?"

Cedric seemed a very pleasant old man, so the two brothers sat at the table while he made them a cup of tea.

Mitch took up the story. "Well, you see it all started when Billy Rabbit said that there was always treasure at the end of a rainbow, so we jumped on our magic bicycle and we've been following it ever since."

"Oh, I see. So you think there is treasure here in

this cave."

Titch looked at Mitch, and said, "We think there might be. Have you found any?"

"Oh yes, you are quite right. There is a very valuable treasure in this cave. See if you can find it."

Titch and Mitch clapped their hands and looked excited.

Cedric spoke again. "If you can find the treasure you can take it away with you. However, if I have to tell you where it is, then it will have to stay here with me. Does that sound fair?"

"Very fair," said Mitch delighted at such an easy offer. "And very kind."

The pixies searched high and low, but they could not find any treasure. They went through all of Cedric's possessions. Titch looked under his bed and Mitch peered into every corner of his wardrobe. Mitch climbed up on his brother's shoulders and checked out all the nooks and crannies at the top of the cave. They discovered other caves linked to the hermit's home, so using Cedric's lamp they explored every one. Finally, they tried the area around the waterfall but they got covered in spray and their clothes became even wetter then before. Eventually, they gave up and, feeling very tired indeed, returned

to Cedric.

"Can you give us a clue?" asked Mitch, a bit dejected. "Do we have to dig for it, because we can't see it anywhere?"

"There is no need to dig for it, but I must say, you have seen it, but you didn't recognise it. Try again."

So, the two pixies looked ever so carefully through all the caves again, but there was no treasure to be found, not a single sparkling jewel or even a small gold coin.

Defeated, they returned to Cedric and Titch said, "We give up. Please tell us where the

treasure is."

The hermit eased himself out of his chair and said, "Come with me."

He led them to an alcove where a bright light shone on an open book resting on a table.

"There," he said proudly, "is the treasure."

"But it's just a book!" exclaimed Titch.

"It's not just any book, it's an encyclopaedia of knowledge. That is more valuable than any pot of gold or chest full of treasure. Tell me, do you know why caterpillars turn into butterflies?"

Titch and Mitch looked at each other. "No," they said together.

"Do you know why it snows when it gets cold?"

"No."

"Do you know why the sun is so hot?"

Again, the two pixies shook their

heads. "No," they said.

"Did you know that human people have been to the moon and back?"

The pixies looked amazed. "Never!"

"Do you know why water is wet?"

"No," said the pixies again.

"Well, the answers and all the information you could ever need are all here in this book. Isn't that more important than any treasure? Have a look at the book and tell me what you think."

Titch and Mitch sat down at the table and turned the pages of the book. It was full of the most interesting stuff.

Titch turned to Cedric and smiling happily said, "This is indeed a wonderful book. We would love to take it back to our own house and read it every day."

"I am so sorry, but I'm afraid the book has to stay here. I did say you could keep it if you found it, but you didn't find it. However, you can come and see me whenever you want, the book will always be here and you can consult it at any time."

"Oh, thank you," said the pixies. It really was a fabulous book and they wished they had spotted it earlier, but they had never thought of a book as being a treasure.

"Just one more thing," said Cedric. "You travelled a long way to get here, do you know where you are?"

Again, the two pixies looked at each other with surprise. "Well, actually, no. We don't know where we are," said Titch.

"And do you know how to get home?"

"No," the pixies spoke in small voices as they realised that they had been so intent on finding the end of the rainbow that they were totally lost.

"That's another valuable thing you'll find in the book," said Cedric. "If you turn to the back page, you'll find a map that will show you where you are and how to get home. Now, don't you think a book like this is more valuable than a pot of gold?"

"Indeed we do," replied Mitch sincerely. "What

good would treasure be if we could never find our way home ever again?"

"That would be horrid," agreed Titch. "Now we can find our way home and tell all our friends that books can be more valuable than gold."

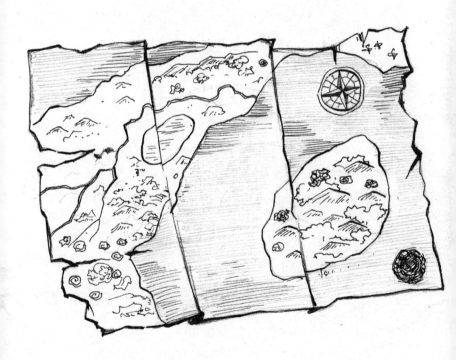

2

The Trolls of Sugar Loaf Wood

TITCH AND MITCH WERE ON THEIR WAY TO
see their friend Misty in Fairy Valley. It was a lovely
sunny morning and the two brothers were riding
their magic bicycle over meadows, fields and the tops
of trees. They were hoping to arrive in Fairy Valley in
time for lunch, when Mitch spotted somebody
waving to them from the top of a tree.

"Look Titch, down there, I see a small person in
a red hat waving to us. Should we fly the bicycle a bit
lower and make sure he's all right?"

"Yes, I see him. Hold tight, I'm going down."

Titch managed to hover the bicycle right over the
top of a big tree, just a few feet from the figure in the

red, pointed hat.

"It's a gnome!" called out Mitch.

Sure enough, just beneath them, a small gnome clung to the very top branch of the tree. He wore a black tunic, red trousers and his face was half covered with a huge white beard.

"Look!" exclaimed Titch. "There, on the ground! What are those creatures and why are they setting fire to the tree?"

Mitch stared hard at the creatures for a few moments. They appeared to be short, fat, little men with long arms, just a bit bigger than the gnome who was clinging to the treetop and staring at them.

"I don't know who they are, but they don't seem very nice. Fancy burning a tree down!"

The voice of the gnome floated up from the top of the tree.

"They are Trolls! Ugly, horrid, vicious, nasty monsters! Setting fire to the tree is the only way to make me come down. Help me, please!"

"We can't," called back Titch. "We can only carry two people on this bicycle and as you can see, there are already two of us here."

The gnome started to wail. "Oh no, they'll catch me and send me down the mine."

Mitch suggested to Titch, "Why don't you drop me off over there on that grassy bank? Then, when you've rescued the gnome, you can come back and collect me. It won't take a minute."

Titch zoomed down to the grassy bank. After Mitch had climbed off the bicycle, he waved to his brother who promptly took off again and headed for the big tree. With a lot of difficulty he managed to hover the bicycle right next to the gnome, who had stopped wailing, but now had tears running down his bright red cheeks.

"Come on," said Titch. "Climb onto the seat behind me."

"I'm too frightened," said the gnome and he clutched at his tree even more firmly. A pall of smoke drifted up to them. "All right," said Titch. "I'll leave you for the trolls. I'm off now, goodbye."

Immediately the gnome loosened his grip on the tree and grabbed at the bicycle before Titch could leave him behind. In a moment, he clambered on to Mitch's seat and hugged Titch round the waist. He then leaned over and shouted down to the watching trolls, "Yah boo, can't catch me. Trolls are horrid, fat monsters and I'm a clever gnome."

Flying the bicycle as fast as he could, Titch landed

on the grassy bank. "Where are you Mitch?" he called out. "We shouldn't hang around here while those trolls are about." Stepping off the bicycle, he looked around.

"Oh dear," said the gnome. "The trolls have probably taken him; there are a lot of them you know. They're all around here and not just under my tree."

"Why do they want Mitch? I don't like to say it, but he can't be much use to them."

Looking at him curiously, the gnome said, "You don't live around here then, do you?"

"No, we live on an island out at sea. I've never even heard of a troll, let alone met one. Who are they?"

"These are the trolls from Sugar Loaf Wood. They are short and fat with long arms and stubby legs. Horrid, ugly things they are."

"Why do they want Mitch?"

"It's not just Mitch. They capture lots of creatures, especially those who can dig."

Sitting down on a rock to rest his aching legs, the gnome explained a little more. "In Sugar Loaf Wood there is a mine called the Sugar Bread Mine. The trolls love to eat sugar bread. That's why they are so fat, it's all they ever eat. The mines are very narrow and the trolls are so fat, they can't squeeze themselves into the mine at all, so they force other creatures to dig out the sugar bread for them. They make the prisoners stay down all the time and only let them out for a glass of water, and before they can drink, they have to give the trolls lots of sugar bread. They really are cruel, those trolls."

Titch was horrified. "Mitch is going down a mine to dig for sugar bread? They can't do that! We must rescue him. Which way did they go?" Titch turned his back on the gnome to look in all directions for

any sign of Mitch.

"WE?" shouted the gnome. "WE must go and rescue Mitch? You must be mad! I'm not going anywhere near those trolls. I'm off."

Titch turned to the gnome angrily, "It's all your fault that the trolls have captured Mitch." But the gnome was

already running down the hill with his red hat bobbing as he went, faster and faster, until he darted into the wood at the bottom of the hill and disappeared for ever.

Titch looked all around him for some sign of the trolls, but there was nothing moving and nobody to be seen anywhere. However, a few metres down the

slope he saw the magic feather that Mitch always wore in his hat. "That confirms it," he said to himself. "Mitch must have been taken by surprise before he could use the feather to defend himself." It was a special feather from a hawk's tail that gave out a bright, scary light when it was waved. Titch put it safely into his pocket and, scratching his head in despair, wondered what to do next.

"Well," he thought, "if the gnome was so frightened of the trolls then he would run as far away from them as he could. So, if I fly in the opposite direction to the gnome, then I'm probably going in the same direction as the trolls." Satisfied with this reasoning, Titch jumped on to the bicycle and called out, "Up, up and away."

Once he was flying as high as he could, he found he could see a long way in every direction. There were fields and woods and streams and hills, but no sign of the trolls. "They can't have travelled very far," he thought. "Perhaps I should fly over the nearest wood, because the trolls might be hidden from view."

Zooming the bicycle low over the nearest wood, Titch peered over the handlebars as he skimmed the treetops. Right in the middle of the wood he came across a clearing with a big hole, like a cave, at one side of it. "Wait a minute," he thought, "that hole could be the entrance to a mine, and that mine could be the Sugar Bread Mine."

He was just about to zoom down and land, when a line of trolls marched into the clearing. A particularly large troll led the way. He swung his long arms as he walked so that his fingers brushed the ground. Titch saw that none of the trolls wore any clothes, but they were covered in thick fur and had big tummies, so they looked like little barrels on short fat legs as they marched along.

The trolls surrounded a group of other creatures who had also been captured. Titch could see another gnome, a beaver, a water rat and a fairy with green

wings and there, amongst the captives, he saw a
pointed green hat.

"There's only one hat like that in the whole
world," he said to himself. "It must be Mitch."

Indeed it was, for as the procession got closer, he
could quite clearly see Mitch himself, underneath the
hat, looking very miserable indeed.

He watched with horror as the trolls, who all had
sharp sticks, poked and jabbed at the prisoners until
they all disappeared down the big hole.

"Oh, my goodness, what shall I do?" he whispered

to himself. Then an idea occurred to him. He needed help and the only creatures he knew for miles around were Misty, who had chickenpox, and Trusty, who would take ages to get here. Then, there was also Wiffen and Perry, who were not far away at all. If Wiffen was supposed to be an intelligent turkey, then he might think of some way to rescue Mitch, and certainly Perry was very big and could be very fierce if he wanted to be. So, turning the bicycle around, he raced away to find the little stone cottage, where Wiffen and Perry lived.

Wiffen and Perry were just settling down to a nice meal of milk, corn and farm scraps, when Titch appeared. On hearing the story of Mitch and the sugar bread trolls, they promised Titch they would do all they could to get him back again.

"Have you any ideas?" asked Wiffen.

"No, that's why I came to you, because you told me you were the most intelligent turkey in the whole world, so please come up with a good idea."

After walking around for a while and scratching his chin, Wiffen finally said, "I believe we need to surprise the trolls. I suggest that we frighten them and when they run away, we rush in and rescue Mitch, and indeed all the other creatures who work down the mine."

"And how do we do that?" Titch asked.

"First of all we sneak through the wood to the mine. There, we hide and wait until all the trolls come out and demand their sugar bread. Then, when the prisoners pop out of the mine, we rush out, frighten the trolls and free the captives!"

"How can a pixie, a turkey and a dog frighten all those trolls?" asked Titch, uncertainly.

"A dog the size of Perry would frighten them, especially when he barks and growls and snarls. If we barked as well, then they would think there were lots of dogs rushing at them. You could wave your sparkly feather, and I can look rather ferocious if I puff up my feathers and spread my wings. You should hear my 'gobble, gobble, gobble' when I'm really angry." Wiffen started to strut around the room puffing and

hissing fiercely.

Titch frowned and said, "How can you bark like a dog and gobble like a turkey all at the same time?"

"I just go 'gobble, bark, gobble, bark, gobble, bark'. Trust me, I'm very talented."

Wiffen looked at Perry thoughtfully and said to him, "We can tie tin cans all over you, put a few pebbles inside them so that when you run they all bang together and make a frightful racket. The more noise the better."

Perry looked alarmed, "I have never bitten anybody in my whole life and I really don't want to bite anyone now, not even a troll. And won't tin cans tied to my fur hurt me?"

"You don't have to bite anyone, just be frightening. The tin cans won't hurt you, and even if they do, it'll make you howl even louder and that would be really frightening."

Perry looked a bit crestfallen. "I suppose so. After all, we have to rescue Mitch."

Wiffen turned to Titch, "As well as barking and waving your sparkly feather, you can bang on this copper pot with a spoon. That makes a horrid noise. So, we come charging out of the wood, barking, growling, snarling, howling, rattling, banging and gobbling. The trolls won't stand a chance! They'll be off screaming with fright and probably stay away all day."

Titch still looked a bit doubtful, but was cheered up by Wiffen's optimism.

"OK," he said. "It might just work. We'll get up early tomorrow and make sure we get there when the trolls gather for their breakfast."

The following morning Titch led the way on the magic bicycle by flying just above the ground and Wiffen rode on Perry's back, clutching onto his fur with his claws. When they reached the wood where the trolls lived, Titch came down to the ground and joined Wiffen and Perry.

"I can't fly the bicycle in the wood, there are too many trees. I'll have to leave it here. We can all charge together when we get to the mine."

Quietly, they walked through the wood and, as they went, Wiffen marked the trees with a white chalk he'd brought with him. "In case we have to run back through the wood, we need to know the way back to the magic bicycle," he explained.

It was just before noon when they arrived at the clearing in the middle of the wood and, peeping out from behind the trees, they saw at least fifteen to twenty trolls milling around. Then, the big troll Titch had seen before, blew a whistle. It was the signal for all prisoners to bring out the sugar bread and before long, a beaver crawled out of the mine carrying a heavy leather bucket. Two gnomes, a rabbit, and a water rat quickly followed him. Then, finally, Mitch

appeared, helping the fairy with green wings who couldn't walk very well.

"Now is the time to charge," announced Wiffen.

"Those trolls have got lots of sharp sticks," said Perry anxiously.

"Go!" shrieked Wiffen, and he pecked Perry on

his bottom quite savagely.

With more of a yelp than a bark, Perry rushed out of the wood. Very quickly, he got into his stride and put together some very loud, fierce barks. Alongside him, and moving very quickly for a plump turkey, Wiffen had his wings stretched out wide as he rushed at the trolls hissing and screeching as loud as he could.

Titch found that he couldn't actually bang the copper pot and wave the hawk's feather at the same time, so he gripped the feather in his mouth and banged on the pot as he raced along.

For a moment, the trolls didn't move. Titch thought that the plan had failed and the trolls would not run away at all. Then, just as they reached the centre of the clearing, Titch dropped the copper pot and, pointing the hawk's feather in front of him, he waved it as hard as he could. A great bright beam of sparkly light shot out and it crackled and spluttered all over the trolls.

It was all too much for them. The sparkly light frightened them and the fierce growls and barks made them think that many dangerous creatures were attacking. The sight of an angry turkey, gobbling and hissing with his wattle bright red and his wings

flapping violently, was the final straw. In one swift movement, the trolls all turned away together and fled to the other side of the clearing where they vanished into the wood. The friends stopped charging and, for a moment, they listened to the noise of the trolls crashing through the trees as they desperately tried to escape the demons they thought were chasing them.

"Hurrah," cried Mitch. "I knew you'd do something, but I didn't expect such a frightening charge out of the woods. It was so terrifying I nearly ran away with the trolls. But then I suddenly recognised Perry in spite of all those tin cans."

"If we've finished

charging, can somebody please take these tin cans off me?" gasped Perry, quite out of breath. Titch obliged and started to cut away the string that held the cans to his fur.

"Where have all the other prisoners gone?" asked Wiffen, looking round the clearing as he puffed and gasped to get his breath back.

"You frightened them so much," said Mitch, "that they all ran away into the wood. But I'm sure they'll find their way home."

They looked at the green fairy, still hanging on to Mitch's arm.

"She's hurt her foot," said Mitch, giving her a warm and reassuring smile.

"And my wings," said the green fairy sadly.

"Her name is Gretel," explained Mitch. "She stopped to help a gnome and the trolls grabbed her. Poor thing has been down the mines for ages and she's very weak."

"She'll have to come with us then," decided Titch.

"Wiffen squawked. "I've just seen a troll peeping at us from behind a tree. Quick, we'd better run."

Immediately Titch and Mitch helped Gretel on to
Perry's back and they all raced into the wood. As
soon as they passed the first tree, a great ROAR went
up from the other side of the clearing. Looking back,
they saw a huge crowd of trolls come charging out of
the trees. This made them run into the wood even
faster and they heard the big troll shout out to the
rest, "Catch them, don't let them get away."

In the dash through the woods, Titch and Mitch
tried to hold Gretel onto Perry's back, but sometimes
he went a bit too fast and twice the poor fairy fell off,
which slowed them down, and let the trolls get
nearer. Wiffen needed to flap his wings to go fast, but
the trees kept getting in his way and he started to fall
behind Perry and the pixies.

The noise of the chasing trolls got louder and louder as they got nearer and nearer. Suddenly, the friends came to a tree with a white chalk mark and Titch gasped. "That's the first tree we marked, the bicycle is just down the path." Then they broke out into the sunshine and they saw the magic bicycle in front of them. Titch and Mitch both grabbed Gretel and swung her down from Perry's back, Titch jumped on to the front seat of the bicycle and Mitch sat on the back seat with Gretel on his knee.

"Oh dear, I hope the bicycle can take the extra weight." Titch was frightened as he heard the roaring of the trolls just behind him.

Turning to look for Wiffen, they saw him break free of the trees with a whole pack of trolls right on his tail feathers. With a final flap of his wings, he gained a little on the trolls and he reached Perry, who had his bottom facing the woods and his head down ready for a quick start when his friend reached him. Wiffen leapt into the air and landed on Perry's back, quickly he dug his claws into the dog's fur and wrapped his wings round Perry's neck. Immediately, Perry bounded forwards and at the same time Titch and Mitch cried out, "Up, up and away."

The bicycle slowly rose off the ground. It was finding the extra weight difficult to manage, but they got high enough off the ground to be just out of reach of the trolls. The trolls were running along right underneath them, jumping up, and snatching at them with their long arms. However, Titch, Mitch and Gretel were safely airborne. In front of them, they could see Perry racing across the meadow with Wiffen hanging on for dear life as they escaped the clutches of the trolls.

Eventually, Perry stopped running as the trolls had been left far behind, so Titch and Mitch landed their bicycle alongside and they congratulated each other in glowing terms.

"Oh Wiffen, you were magnificent," said Mitch. "You could have beaten the trolls single handed."

"And you were the bravest pixie in the whole world," Wiffen said to Titch.

Looking at Perry, Wiffen said, "Did you manage to bite any of the trolls?"

"Of course not. I was too busy barking, growling and howling to do any biting. In fact, I nearly choked trying to do them all at once. It was a good job the trolls ran away when they did."

They all turned to Gretel to see if she was all

right. "How are you?" asked Mitch gently.

"I'm going to be fine, thanks to all of you."

"You must come home with us," said Wiffen. "You can stay at our cottage until your wing mends."

"Thank you," said Gretel. "That's so kind."

Titch and Mitch said goodbye and climbed on to their bicycle. Together they shouted out the magic words, "Up, up and away!"

When they were high in the air and flying over the sea, Mitch tapped his brother on the shoulder

and said, "Oh, I forgot to mention that I saved you a piece of sugar bread from the mine; would you like to taste it?" He pulled a piece of bread from his pocket and handed it to Titch.

"I already hate sugar bread," retorted Titch, "and I never ever want to eat it." As he spoke, he took the piece of bread and threw it as far as he could.

The two pixies watched it float down to the sea and as it hit the water they both cheered loudly.

3

The Day the Stream Ran Dry

IT STARTED VERY EARLY ONE MORNING.
Titch and Mitch had not even had time for their
breakfast, when they heard a commotion outside
their little cottage. Willy Water Rat and his whole
family were running up and down the bank of the
stream in a most agitated state.

The two pixies hurried outside. When they
reached the stream they found it had run dry. Willy
Water Rat came over to them and said, "It just
happened. When I woke up this morning there was
no water. Look at all the poor fish."

Everywhere they looked, fish were flapping around
trying to stay alive in what little water there was.

"Oh my goodness," said Titch. "What shall we do?"

Mitch said thoughtfully, "If we dig holes in the middle of the stream, then the water that is left will flow into them and make safe pools for the fish, at least until the water comes back."

"Right," said Titch, "then we can follow the stream back up the hill and find out where all the water has gone."

"Good idea," exclaimed Willy. "Leave the digging to us."

Titch started running along the bank of the stream shouting, "Come on Mitch."

However, Mitch had other ideas. He hurried back to the cottage, grabbed two sandwiches for breakfast, wrapped them up and went out into the garden to get the magic bicycle. Jumping on he called out, "Up, up and away!"

The bicycle shot up into the air and Mitch steered it along the bank of the stream. He flew over his brother and landed in front of him. When Titch staggered up, panting and already out of breath, Mitch said, "It will be much easier if we use the bicycle, you know."

Too exhausted to say anything, Titch clambered onto the back seat and put his arms round Mitch's waist.

"Up, up and away!" Mitch called out again and made the bicycle hover over the stream for a minute,

then he steered it carefully upstream, studying the
ground below to see if any holes had appeared, which
could have sucked away the water. All they could see
were more and more fish desperately trying to stay
alive in muddy puddles.

They flew over the stream right up to the top of
the hill. "There, look at that!" cried Mitch.

In front of them loomed a dam that had been
built right across the empty stream. It was made of
branches and twigs which, when all piled together,
had stopped the water from flowing down the hill.
However, on the other side of the dam a lake had

formed, which was getting bigger and bigger as more water flowed in.

"It must be the work of beavers," said Titch, peering over Mitch's shoulder at the dam. "Yes, look down there, I can see them swimming about in the lake. Let's go down and talk to them."

The two friends zoomed down and landed by the side of the new lake. Walking up and down the water's edge, they waved to the beavers to try to attract their attention. Eventually, a large, hairy beaver with white

whiskers around a twitching nose swam over to
them, dragged himself out of the water, shaking it off

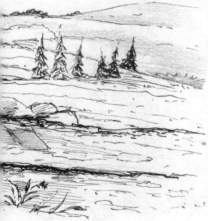

like a dog.

"Who are you?" he asked.
"I have never seen creatures
like you before."

"We are pixies,"
responded Titch.
"Unfortunately, we haven't
time to chat. You have
caused a massive problem
down the hill. The stream

has run dry!"

"Goodness me, we only finished building our dam yesterday. Isn't it a magnificent piece of work?" The white-whiskered beaver sat back on his haunches and waved a paw proudly in the direction of the dam.

"It certainly is, but unfortunately it's got to go." Titch was emphatic.

"Oh no, it hasn't."

"Oh yes, it has." Mitch joined in.

"Oh no, it hasn't."

"Oh yes, it has!" Both pixies shouted together.

"Oh no, it hasn't!" The beaver smacked his wide, heavy tail down on the ground and sniffed with irritation. Then he said, "Why?"

By this time, Titch had become so angry that he was speechless.

Mitch, who was always easygoing and very slow to take offence, took over and said, "By the way, my name is Mitch and my brother here is called Titch."

"Pleased to meet you, I'm sure. I'm called Whiskers," sniffed the beaver.

"If you'll come with me, I'll show you the problem," Mitch said, and, leading the beaver to the side of the dam, they peered over the edge and looked down the hill.

"Oh dear," said Whiskers. "There's no water in the stream at all. What's gone wrong? I don't understand, whenever I build a dam, only some of the water goes into the lake, then, when it's finished, the water overflows round the side here and fills up the stream again. But if the stream has run dry, then where's all the water going?"

"That's what we've come here to find out."

Titch found his voice, "There are tons of fish in trouble all the way down the stream. When the puddles dry up, they'll die."

Whiskers thought for a moment. "Come with me," he said. "I've got a small raft here. If you two will jump on board, I'll take you all round the edges of our new lake and we'll see if we can find where the water is going."

Titch and Mitch climbed onto the raft and Whiskers set off, using a pole to push it through the water. On the other side of the lake, they found the problem. The water had filled up the lake all right, but now it was overflowing through a gap in the rocks on the other side and cascading down the hill a long way from where it should be.

"Leave this to me," said Whiskers. "I'll get the family over here straight away and we'll fill that gap. Once that is done, the water will go round the dam where it is supposed to go, you'll see. Come on, let's get back to your bicycle."

When they returned, they were horrified to see the mischievous young beavers playing with their precious bicycle. As they weren't the right shape to ride it properly, they had dragged the bicycle into the

water and were swimming all over and around it."

"No," cried Titch, "leave it alone you rascals."

"Come on you lot," shouted Whiskers. "Leave that thing alone. We've got work to do, grab some twigs and follow me. This is an emergency."

In a flash, all the beavers dived after Whiskers and left Titch and Mitch to drag their bicycle out of the lake. Heaving it out, they set it aside and Mitch began to dry it off.

"First things first Mitch," said Titch, stopping him. "Let's try to get some water flowing down the hill. Those beavers might be a while plugging that gap."

They grabbed some long sticks and started to poke at the side of the dam from where the water was supposed to flow. It didn't take them long to clear the earth and twigs away, then, with a sudden rush, water poured through the gap. They stood back and watched it flow back into the stream.

"Well done!" cried Mitch. "That should keep those fish alive until the beavers finish their work."

By now, they were tired, wet and covered in mud, so they made their way over to their bicycle and sat down beside it.

"We might as well go home now," said Titch. "Do you want to steer the bike?"

"Of course," said Mitch. "All aboard."

Settling themselves on their seats, they called out together, "Up, up and away!" But nothing happened. The magic bicycle didn't move at all.

After they walked round and round the bicycle, scratching their heads and wondering what to do, they decided that maybe the bicycle didn't like the soaking it had had in the lake.

"Oh, I do hope it works when it dries out," said Titch. "It's a wonderful bicycle."

"Perhaps it's only magic for a few days," Mitch

said thoughtfully.

"Surely not! Misty would have said something if there was going to be a problem. We'll just have to wait until it dries off, then we can try again. The sun is shining now, so it won't take long."

There was nothing more they could do except sit and wait. Every now and again, one of them would walk over to the magic bicycle and turn it round so that all it's parts were exposed to the warmth of the sun.

The beavers must have been very busy plugging the gap in the rocks, because while they were waiting, the flow down to the stream increased steadily as more water swirled round the side of the dam. Suddenly, Whiskers' head appeared out of the water and he called out to them, "How's the water

flowing? Have we saved the fish?"

Titch responded, "Yes, we must have. It's flowing by the gallon now. We want to go and have a look, but our bicycle doesn't work any more."

"I'll give it another go," said Mitch. He walked over to the bicycle and examined it closely, then called to Titch, "It's dry now. Keep your fingers crossed!"

Mitch clambered onto the front seat and said the magic words yet again, "Up, up, and away!"

This time the magic bicycle responded and rose into the air, slowly at first, but then it gathered speed and finally Mitch was able to make it zoom all round the lake, before landing beside Titch.

"Thank goodness the magic has come back," Titch said. "But it looks as though the bicycle loses some of its magic when it gets wet."

Titch climbed up behind Mitch and, with a wave to Whiskers and his family, they hovered over the stream again and this time they went down the hill and back to their home. All the way down the stream was filling right up to its banks and life was getting back to normal.

They landed in the garden of their cottage and rushed out to the riverbank. A worn out Willy Water

Rat and his family were sitting with a large number of frogs watching the water rush down the stream. A large fish jumped out of the water and waved its tail at them before diving back into the stream and swimming away.

"Well done," said Willy when he saw them. "We couldn't dig any more holes. You got the water back just in time."

4
Wendy

THE FIRST TIME TITCH AND MITCH VISITED
a town where human people lived was on Titch's
birthday. As a treat, Titch had said he wanted to use
the magic bicycle and fly over the town that Budgie
had told them about.

"It's a pretty town," she had said. "Situated on the
coast, just over a mile away, so it's easy to find.
There's a little harbour, where fishing boats come and
go, and a church with a steeple that stretches high
into the sky. But, my favourite spot is a jam factory
on the edge of the town. It has loads and loads of
strawberries, plums, raspberries, peaches and lots
more. If I am quick, and I usually am," she'd boasted,

"I fly in very low and very fast, then with a snatch of my beak, I can get away with a delicious piece of fruit." Looking at the magic bicycle doubtfully, she'd added, "It's a nice bicycle, but I don't think it will be quick enough to snatch some fruit."

"That doesn't matter," Titch had replied. "We are not going to eat any fruit; all we want to do is to fly over, have a look around and come back home."

Although it was a nice day when they set off, the clouds were gathering overhead without the two pixies noticing. They had reached the town and were looking down at all the people, the cars, and the buses, when a bolt of lightning suddenly sizzled across the sky and they nearly fell off the bicycle with surprise. Titch, who was steering, wrestled with the

handlebars and soon set the magic bicycle back on a steady course.

"My goodness," exclaimed Mitch. "Look at those black clouds. There's going to be a thunderstorm and the lightning might hit us next time!"

"What are we going to do?" wailed Titch. "We have to land somewhere quickly."

In vain, they looked around for a quiet area of level ground, but all they could see were houses, cars, roads and more houses.

Suddenly, the rain started. Great big drops splashed all over them and then it came down faster and faster until they were both soaking wet. Unable to fly in the rain, the magic bicycle started to fall lower until it just skimmed the rooftops. Finally, it dropped like a stone out of the sky with the two pixies clutching each other and squealing loudly with fright.

CRASH! The magic bicycle landed heavily on the wet roof of a small house. It skidded along the slippery tiles until it banged into a chimney and, finally, came to a stop.

"Phew! That was close!" said Mitch.

"We'd better dismount before this thing falls any further. You first," cautioned Titch, "but tread carefully."

With the bicycle leaning precariously against the chimney pot, Mitch gingerly stepped off, then held the bike steady for Titch to follow.

Looking around, Titch noticed a television aerial poking up beside the chimney. Perfect, he thought.

"Give me your belt," he said to Mitch.

"What for?" replied Mitch, alarmed.

"I need it to tie the bike to the aerial, so that it doesn't fall off the roof," said Titch.

Mitch shook his head.

"No." he said, firmly. "My trousers will fall down. Use your own belt."

"I don't have a belt; my trousers are tight enough

without one." As Titch spoke, he held on to the
bicycle with one hand and the chimney pot with the
other and all the time the rain kept pouring down
until they were soaked to the skin.

With great reluctance, Mitch unbuckled his belt
and handed it over to Titch, who quickly tied the
bicycle to the television aerial so it wouldn't fall off
the roof. The two pixies then sat on the edge of the
chimney pot with their feet dangling inside and got
wetter and wetter.

Suddenly, another bolt of lightning and a great
clap of thunder joined together and crashed across

the sky. With a yelp of fright, the pixies grabbed each other, jumped up in the air and fell down the chimney.

Rolling and tumbling, the two brothers hurtled down through the dark until, battered and bruised, they landed with a thud in the fireplace below. Crawling out, they found themselves on the soft, beige carpet of a fair sized room with large windows and orange curtains. The walls were decorated with pictures of teddy bears, fairies and, to their amazement, pixies.

For a moment, they forgot how wet and bedraggled they were and began to explore the room, leaving tiny, wet footprints all over the otherwise spotless carpet. The first thing that attracted their attention, was a hot radiator under the nearest window. A nearby chair made it easy for them to clamber up to the top of the radiator. Titch went first, then he pulled Mitch up behind him and, before long, they were drying off nicely. The radiator, however was just a little bit too hot for them and soon began to burn their feet, so they hopped and danced up and down.

"Look at that, Mitch." Titch pointed to a dolls house in the middle of the room.

"What a magnificent little house," said Mitch, as he hopped from one foot to another, panting with the effort. "I wonder who lives here."

"I think it's the room of a little girl," said Titch, pointing. "Look, there's a photograph of a little girl

on the window ledge behind you."

Mitch turned round and looked at the framed
picture. It was a picture of a girl dressed in a school
uniform with a bag over her shoulder and looking
very proud. On the wall, next to the window, was a

painting of a big flower in very bright colours. This caught Mitch's eye and in the bottom left hand corner he saw a name written in thick blue letters.

"Wendy. Six and three quarters," he read. Then, turning to Titch, he said, "I think her name is 'Wendy'."

Just then, the door opened and before the two pixies could hide, a little girl walked in clutching a doll to her chest. She was a little older than six and three quarters, perhaps nearer seven and a half, with short, curly, fair hair and large blue eyes. She wore a

white dress decorated with red stripes, white socks pulled up to her knees and little pink shoes. Under her arm she carried a small doll, which wore a red dress with white stripes, red socks and also pink shoes. The girl and the doll matched each other perfectly.

As soon as the little girl saw the two pixies hopping up and down on the radiator, she dropped the doll, clapped her hand over her mouth and let out a muffled screech. Her eyes opened wide with shock and she turned to rush out of the room.

"Please don't go," called out Titch. "We're only two pixies trying to get dry."

"You must be Wendy," said Mitch, smiling in the most friendly way he could think of. "Please don't be frightened. My name is Mitch and this is my brother, Titch. Please excuse our jigging about like this, but the radiator is too hot for our feet and we're only trying to get dry."

"Actually," added Titch, "I think we've dried off enough now."

The two brothers ran to the end of the radiator and jumped onto a chair.

Wendy looked at them in astonishment, but instead of running away, her curiosity won over her

fear and she said in a whisper, "Are you really pixies? I didn't know there were any real pixies? Where did you come from? How did you get here?"

Titch replied, "We certainly are pixies and we live

on an island not far away. Unfortunately, we got caught in the rain and fell down your chimney."

"You see," added Mitch, "our bicycle doesn't work in the rain."

Wendy came over to the chair where the two pixies stood and, reaching out with both hands, she grasped them firmly round the waist, lifted them off the chair and placed them by her doll's house.

Having got over the shock of finding pixies in her room, she was now keen to make them welcome. Titch and Mitch were amazed when Wendy opened up the front of the little house to reveal a lounge, a kitchen, two bedrooms and a set of stairs at the back. The whole house was fitted out in the most elegant and comfortable style.

"Please stay here," she said. "You can live in my dolls house if you like."

"It's a bit small," said Titch, peering inside.

"We already have a house at home, thank you very much," added Mitch, not really wanting to move house just yet.

However, overcome by curiosity, the two stepped carefully into the dolls house, impressed by the alluring soft furnishings.

"This is a very nice home," said Titch, crouching

on the sofa to avoid banging his head on the ceiling. "I think I could get used to it."

Mitch was more doubtful, but said nothing and simply sat in the nearest armchair, which turned out to be much less comfortable than it looked.

"You can share it with my dolls. They'd love to have some company," Wendy said with delight and she brought in the doll she had been carrying. "This is Jemma," she said by way of introduction, placing the rigid doll on the chair next to Mitch. Then she stepped back and clapped her hands with glee. "What a lovely couple you make! I think you should get married right away."

Mitch glowered at Jemma, who simply sat there with a fixed smile.

"I don't think so," he replied, looking the motionless doll up and down. "She's not really my type."

On the sofa, Titch sniggered and said, "What a good idea Mitch, it's time you got married."

"You can marry Jemma then," retorted Mitch. "I'm not."

Wendy chipped in, "Oh no, he can't marry Jemma because he's going to marry Chloe!" Wendy rushed over to a box at the end of the room and came back with another plastic doll with fair hair, blue eyes and a fixed smile. Placing the doll next to Titch, she said. "This is Chloe. Say hello."

Titch mumbled a greeting. Chloe said nothing.

Wendy was thrilled. "Now you can all live happily ever after."

Titch stood up and, banging his head on the ceiling, promptly sat down again.

"I do hate to spoil your happy ending," he said, putting on his best sad face, "but I'm not sure my

brother and I are quite ready to get married.

However, if we could rest here until it stops raining, that would be very kind."

"Perhaps we could have a cup of tea and a slice of cake?" added Mitch, hopefully.

Just then, a voice called from somewhere outside the room. "Wendy?" it said, "Where are you?"

"In my bedroom, Mummy," Wendy answered, turning to the door. Feet could be heard coming up the stairs.

Turning back to the pixies, Wendy whispered, "Just stay in the dolls house. Mummy is short sighted so she won't notice you."

"That's all right, Wendy," said Titch, standing up again, but keeping his head low to avoid the ceiling. "Mitch and I would love to meet a fully grown human person, so we'd like to say hello to your mummy." Titch was always keen to make new friends.

The door opened and a slender woman with a

pretty face entered the room. She was wearing a striped green apron and smiling happily. In her hands she carried a small tray, which she placed on a side table. On it stood a glass of milk and a strawberry tart.

"There you are, my dear, it's time for your glass of milk." Stepping back, she folded her arms and beamed at her daughter.

"Mummy, I've got two new friends whose names are Titch and Mitch. They're pixies you know, and they would like to meet you."

Titch and Mitch stepped out of the dolls house to say hello, but before they could utter a single word, Wendy's mother screamed and shouted in a shrill voice, "Rats! Rats! There are rats in the room!"

Grabbing her daughter, she raced out of the room, still screaming and dragging Wendy by the arm.

Titch shouted out, "We're not rats, we're pixies!" But it was no use, Wendy and her mother had gone.

They did not stay gone for long though. A moment later Wendy's mother was back, carrying a long handled broom and growling ominously. "Where are those rats?" she said, scouring the room for any sign of movement.

The little girl was crying, hanging on to her

mother's dress and shouting, "They're not rats, they're pixies!"

The broom was wafted and poked all around the room as Wendy's mother searched for the two pixies.

By now, Titch and Mitch were hiding in the bedroom of the dolls' house and peeping out of the window as the broom was poked under the chairs, behind the curtains and under the table. When Wendy's mother turned the broom round and poked the handle into every room of the dolls' house, they decided it was time to leave. Darting out of the back door, they raced to where Wendy stood by the bedroom door.

As soon as she saw them, Wendy bent down and picked up the pixies again, one in each hand. Unfortunately, her mother saw her do it and screamed out, "Drop those rats, Wendy. Let me whack them!"

It was all too much for the two pixies. "Try the hawk's feather," said Titch to Mitch.

Taking the feather out of his hat, Mitch pointed it at the angry mother and waved it gently. Immediately, a sparkly light flashed out and covered Wendy's mother in a white light, which crackled and

fizzed and made her hair stand on end. With a loud screech, Wendy's mother raced out of the room.

"She'll be back," said Titch, and wriggling round in Wendy's hand he called to her, "We'd better be going. If you would be so kind as to let us out of the window, we'll be on our way."

Wendy went to the window and, placing the pixies on the sill, opened the window so that they could climb out onto the ledge.

"Please come down my chimney again will you?" she said, with a small tear in her eye. "I'll tell my mummy all about you and next time she won't try to whack you with a broom."

However, just as she spoke, her mother stormed back into the room, grabbed Wendy from behind and pulled the window shut so hard that the two brothers lost their footing and fell.

Luckily, their fall was broken by a bed of soft, bouncy heather. Scrambling to their feet, Titch and Mitch rushed across the lawn and hid behind a prickly rose bush. As they peeped out to see if it was safe to move, Titch said, "At least it's stopped raining. All we have to do is climb up to the top of the house and we can get away on the magic bicycle."

"And how, may I ask, do we climb to the top of the house?" said Mitch, with a worried look on his face.

Titch shaded his eyes from the sun and stared long and hard at the side of the house and said, "There's a drainpipe that goes up the side of the house, past the bedroom window and joins up with a gutter on the roof. If we can climb up it and crawl along the tiles we'll reach the bicycle."

"Oh dear," said Mitch, frowning. "I don't like climbing; if I get too high I get very frightened, my mouth goes all dry and my legs start to tremble."

"Don't worry, you can go first and I'll be right behind you. Go on, it's the only way we can get home."

Mitch approached the drainpipe and wrapped his arms around it. Then he put his left foot on the brick wall behind the drainpipe and lifted his body off the ground. His right foot followed suit and slowly he walked a few steps up the side of the house.

Titch, following close behind, was very impressed and said encouragingly, "Well done, that's the way and if you don't look down you'll be fine."

But when he came level with the bedroom window, Mitch couldn't help looked about him. There was a lovely view, but Mitch didn't notice it. He suddenly became rigid with fear and stopped climbing altogether.

"Go on," called out Titch from beneath him. "Close your eyes and climb. We're nearly there."

"I can't." Mitch replied and he grabbed the drainpipe so tight that his legs started to wobble and he lost his footing. Unfortunately, his shaking legs made his trousers fall down and they dropped right over Titch's head.

"Get them off me," called out Titch in a muffled voice. "I can't see a thing."

"I can't. I daren't let go of the drainpipe. You shouldn't have made me take my belt off."

The pixies started to slide down the drainpipe. As they slipped slowly past the bedroom window again, it suddenly opened and Wendy's head poked out. She looked at them anxiously and reached out a hand to Mitch. "Grab hold of my hand

quick before you fall," she said.

He grabbed it and Wendy eased him onto the window ledge where he looked down at the ground. He gave a gasp of horror and climbed quickly up Wendy's arm, over her head, and disappeared into the house.

Titch followed suit, with Mitch's trousers still wrapped around his shoulders, and soon two very relieved pixies sat on the floor of Wendy's bedroom, right back where they started. When they had recovered their composure, and Mitch his clothing, they explained to Wendy why they had to get to the top of the house.

"Maybe I can help," said Wendy, thoughtfully. "Mummy has got a headache and gone for a lie down in her bedroom. There's a roof window in the loft. Would that help?"

"It certainly would," replied Mitch.

"Right then. You sit on my shoulders and I'll take you up to the loft."

The two pixies made themselves comfortable on Wendy's shoulders and held on to the little girl's hair to keep their balance. She then tiptoed past the door to her mother's room and up some creaky stairs to the loft. Once inside, Wendy moved a chair to stand

on, so that she could reach the handle of the window. Unfortunately, it was just too stiff for her to move.

"Try harder," whispered Mitch.

"I am trying hard. It just won't move."

"Let me help."

Wendy balanced Mitch on her head and then she reached up and grasped the handle again. This time Mitch could also reach the handle, so the two of them heaved down on it, but it still wouldn't budge.

"Why don't you turn the key?" said Titch,
noticing that the handle had a key in it.

"Good idea," said Mitch. Wendy turned the key,
unlocked the window and opened it.

Slowly, Titch and Mitch crawled out onto the
damp roof. Just above them was the magic bicycle,
still strapped to the television aerial.

As they started their ascent up the sloping roof,
Titch turned round to wave to Wendy who was
watching them anxiously from the open window.
"Goodbye," he called. "Thank you for saving us. We
promise to come back and see you again. Goodbye."

Wendy waved back and, hearing her mother's
voice calling again, closed the window hurriedly.

Titch got to the bicycle first, then turned round

to help his brother. Mitch was crawling slowly up the roof, hampered by his trousers, which were starting to

fall down again and getting tangled around his knees. "I'm stuck," he called up to Titch. "I need my belt."

Climbing onto the magic bicycle and holding firmly onto the television aerial, Titch untied the belt and let it slide down the roof towards Mitch. "Watch out Mitch, here it comes."

The belt whizzed down the sloping roof and ended up wrapped around Mitch's neck. Gingerly, he rolled on to his back and pulled up his trousers. When he had the belt back in place, he started back up the roof.

Reaching Titch, he jumped up behind him and, with fingers crossed, they called out together, "Up, up and away!" Immediately, and much to their great relief, the bicycle rose up into the air and, heading for the coast, soon left the chimney pot and the rest of Wendy's house far behind.

"Next year," said Titch to Mitch, "I'm going to stay at home for my birthday!"

5

The Little Green Tree

ONE MORNING MITCH OPENED THE FRONT door of the cottage and got the surprise of his life. There, growing by the side of the path, was a little green tree. He stood and stared at it for a very long moment with his mouth wide open. There had been no trees growing on their path yesterday. Calling out to Titch, he cried, "Look at this! Come quickly and look at this tree."

"Oh, my goodness," exclaimed Titch, as he joined his brother in the doorway and stared at the little green tree. "Where did that come from?"

"I don't know. I can't imagine. Trees don't grow overnight."

Stepping into the garden, the pixies walked round and round the tree. It was only a baby tree, a mere sapling, but it was still bigger than they were.

"It looks a bit like a Christmas tree," said Mitch, thoughtfully.

"Yes," agreed Titch, "but the branches are very close together and the needles are soft and quite small. I really don't know what kind of a tree it is."

They prodded the tree and pushed it, but it was very solid and rooted firmly into the ground.

"What shall we do with it?" asked Mitch.

"Nothing," replied Titch. "We can't cut it down, so it will just have to stay here. I wonder if it's a magic tree that grew very quickly. Or, maybe somebody dug it up from the woods and planted it in our garden during the night."

For the rest of the day, as they went about their business, they gradually got used to the tree being there, and by the time evening came, had grown quite fond of it.

The next day, Titch was up early and peeped out of the window. The little green tree was still in the garden, but to his enormous surprise, it was growing in a different place. In fact, it was now so close to the front door, they couldn't get out of the house.

"Come quickly Mitch," he called out. "The tree has moved."

They had to use the back door and run round to

the front of the house to see the little green tree.
They stood and looked at the tree for ages,
scratching their heads and wondering how it could
have moved during the night. Did somebody dig it up
and plant it even closer to the house? It really was a
mystery. They watched it all through the day, but the

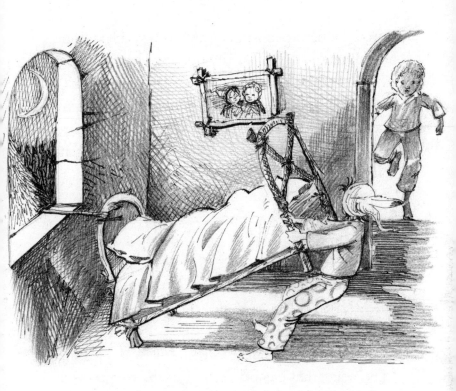

little green tree stayed firmly fixed in the ground.

It was in the evening when Mitch had an idea. "Perhaps we should tie some string around the trunk of the tree, and tie the other end to the leg of a bed. Then, if the tree moves again during the night, the bed will move, wake us up and we will see who is moving it."

"What a good idea!" exclaimed Titch.

So they tied a string around the tree, passed it

through the bedroom window and fastened it to the leg of Mitch's bed.

That evening, Mitch was about to climb into his bed, when it suddenly whizzed across the room and crashed into the wall under the window.

"The tree is on the move," shouted Mitch. "Come quick."

The two pixies raced to the front door and opened it. There, at the end of the path, was the little green tree lying on its side with its roots pointing everywhere.

As Titch and Mitch ran up to it, they became aware of a sobbing noise and realised that the tree was crying.

"Are you all right, Little Green Tree?" said Mitch.

The voice that came from within the tree was soft and quiet. "Somebody tripped me up. It is not easy trying to run on my roots. In fact, it hurts and I don't like it."

"Why are you running on your roots?" asked Titch. "I've never known a tree to move around like you do."

"I'm sorry you fell over," said Mitch, hurriedly untying the string. "But we only wanted to know why you moved around our garden each day."

"Because of the witch of course! I'm frightened of the witch and I'm hiding from her. I know she's going to find me sooner or later. What am I going to do?" The little green tree started to cry again. This time, tears started to drip off the end of some of its branches.

"What witch?" said Titch in surprise. "There's no

witch on this island."

"Oh, yes there is, and she's not a nice witch at all. In fact, she's a horrid witch and I've got to hide."

"Why is she after you?" asked Mitch.

"She wants me for a spell. I heard her say she has looked everywhere for the roots of a little green tree. She wants my roots to make a special spell."

"How awful," said Titch. "How did she find you?"

"One evening, just before dark, the witch came zooming into the wood on a broomstick. As soon as she saw me, she landed, stood up and shouted out, 'At last, a little green tree that is just the right size.' It was horrible. Then she pointed a long, knobbly finger

at me and shouted again, 'I want your roots little tree, right now.' Then she stretched her arms out wide, looked up at the sky and made a spell by shouting:

'Hoots, coots, toots and moots.

Pick up your roots and use them like boots.'

I felt my roots start to wriggle in the ground and before I knew it, they were all loose, so to stop falling over I picked them up out of the ground and ran away using my roots just like legs. However, they were all loose and floppy and I kept tottering all over the path. When the witch came after me, my mummy, who was growing right next to me, swished

a branch and knocked the witch over."

"You poor little tree," said Titch, who was amazed that a witch would do such a thing. "What happened next?"

"I ran away as fast as I could, and before the witch could catch me, it got dark. Then, I tiptoed out of the wood and came across your little house, so I thought I would hide in your garden. I wriggled my roots into the ground and hoped the witch wouldn't find me."

Titch was puzzled. "But you moved right up to our front door the next day. Why?"

"I was even more frightened, so I got as close to the house as I could. The wicked witch only looks for me during the day, so last night I tried to find a better hiding place, but I couldn't find one anywhere so I came back to your cottage."

"If the witch can't find you in the woods, she'll come and look for you here and she's bound to see you sitting in the garden," said Mitch.

Titch looked at Mitch and said, "I think Little Green Tree should come inside the house until we can think of a better hiding place."

"Of course," agreed Mitch. "That's a great idea.

Come on Little Green Tree, we'll help you get inside."

"Oh thank you, but please don't stand on my roots, they are still very sore from falling over."

Between them, Titch and Mitch managed to get the tree upright and pushed it through the front door and into the lounge, where it promptly fell onto the sofa and let out a sigh of relief. "Oh that's much better. That witch won't find me here."

Unfortunately, the little green tree was wrong. The witch did find it. Around about midday, a shadow passed over the window and suddenly the witch's face peered in. Mitch squealed with surprise and stared at it with horror. The witch was dressed all in black, but her large face was very pale and bony with a long, pointed nose.

"Come out little tree! I want your roots for a very special spell." Her voice was loud and harsh.

"You can't come in, the door is locked," shouted Titch nervously.

"Locks don't bother me," roared the witch, and she pulled out a magic wand.

"Quick Mitch!" said Titch. "Use your magic feather."

Mitch always wore the hawk's feather which Misty, the fairy, had made magic, in his hat. Grabbing it, he pointed it straight out in front of him, directly at the witch's face. As soon as he waved it, a beam of light filled the window. The witch gave quite a yelp and jumped backwards.

"Magic pixies are you? Well, I've got a spell to deal with that."

Prowling up and down the garden, the witch muttered to herself, "'Snitch, snatch, scruffle and

scratch...' Oh, what is that dratted spell? 'Bucket of bile and all things vile...' I can't remember it! There are too many spells to remember," grumbled the witch to herself. "I'll have to go and look it up in my book."

She turned to face the house again and shouted, "You look after those roots little tree. I'll be back as soon as I find the spell that turns pixies into toads." Then she grabbed her broomstick, flew up into the sky, and disappeared.

"Oh my, oh my!" said Mitch. "What are we going to do? The witch is going to turn us into toads!"

"I don't believe she can," said Titch boldly. "Your magic feather won't let her get near enough."

"I don't want to wait to find out. We have to hide

as well," said Mitch. "Where can we go?"

The two pixies sat and thought very hard. Then, Titch jumped up with a cry, "I know! There's that cave in the cliffs just by the beach. You have to paddle out and round the corner to find it, but we should be safe there. That witch would never think of paddling out to sea to look for Little Green Tree."

"I can't paddle out to sea!" said Little Green Tree in alarm.

"Don't worry, we'll help you. It's not very far."

"No, the sea water is salt water. My roots would die in salty water. That wouldn't work."

Titch's face fell, then it brightened up again as he thought of another idea. "There's a plastic bag in the garden. You remember Mitch, it was washed up on the beach and we kept it. I think we could put Little Green Tree's roots into the plastic bag and tie the top high up round its trunk, then we could help it through the sea water and keep its roots dry."

Mitch agreed. "What a good idea!" Turning to Little Green Tree he added, "Don't worry, we can put the bag over your roots when we get to the edge of the water. It's not very far to the cave from there. You'll be fine."

With Titch and Mitch walking on either side of

Little Green Tree, they made their way to the beach. It was rather slow, because the little tree's roots were not used to walking and the two pixies had to support it and help it along.

All the time they kept looking around and hoping that the witch wouldn't come back while they were making their way to the beach. Finally, they managed to get to the top of the cliffs and support the little tree down the winding path and on to the sand. When they reached the water's edge, Titch said, "Look, Little Green Tree, the cave is just round that

corner!" Titch pointed towards a rock at the end of the beach.

Laying Little Green Tree on the ground, Titch and Mitch unfolded the plastic bag, carefully placed the roots inside and tied the top tightly round its lower branches. It was a very good fit. Then, after helping Little Green Tree back on to its roots, the two pixies set out to walk through the water and round to the cave.

"The water is cold," said Mitch with a shriek.

"Keep a tight hold on Little Green Tree, and forget about the cold," ordered Titch.

Slowly, they made their way through the sea until the waves lapped around their waists. Then Little Green Tree started to cry. "It's too deep, we're going to drown," it wailed.

Titch looked over his shoulder to make sure the witch was nowhere in sight. Up in the sky he saw a black spot.

"Hurry up. I think the witch is coming."

Little Green Tree nearly fell over as they splashed as fast as they could through the water. Just as they saw the entrance to the cave, they heard a wild shriek right above them. The witch, in her black robes, hovered on her broomstick in front of them

and blocked their way into the cave.

"IDIOTS!" roared the witch. "Don't you know that sea water will kill the roots of a tree? They are no use to me now!"

The angry witch turned a complete somersault on her broomstick and came to rest in front of the pixies. She had her magic wand in her hand and, snarling, she cried, "Stupid pixies! You've ruined my spell! You've destroyed the tree I wanted, so you both deserve to be turned into toads!" Raising her wand into the air, she started to chant a spell, "'Shrink and shrivel, twist and swivel...'"

But that was as far as she got. Pulling the magic feather from his hat, Mitch pointed it as fast as he could at the witch. He was so quick that the feather threw out a light that crackled and hissed far more

than it had ever done before. It seemed that the
feather knew it needed a very strong light indeed.
The result surprised them. For a very long moment
the witch was covered from head to toe in the magic
beam. Then her pale face turned bright red, her hat
fell off and her hair stood on end. With a very loud
screech she spun round on her broomstick.

"Again, Mitch, do it again!" shouted Titch.

So Mitch pulled back his arm and thrust the
feather towards the upside down witch. Once again,
the crackly light streamed out and covered her from
toe to head. It was too much for the witch and she
flew as fast as she could away from the two pixies and

Little Green Tree. The last they saw of her was a small, black dot in the distance.

"Well done, Mitch!" cried Titch with relief. "That really is a fearsome feather."

Little Green Tree said, "That silly witch didn't know I had a plastic bag over my roots, which has kept them perfectly dry."

"I think we can go home now," said Titch. "That witch won't come back to our island in a hurry. Turning us into toads indeed! I don't think so."

Wading back to the beach, they helped Little Green Tree out of the plastic bag and then started the journey back to their cottage.

When they finally got home, they left Little Green Tree in the garden and walked into the wood looking for the place where it used to live. After a while, they found a big green tree that looked like a large Christmas tree, standing next to a small hole in the ground. Titch looked at it and said to Mitch, "This big tree looks just like Little Green Tree. I wonder if that hole is where it picked up its roots and ran away?"

A voice boomed out of the big tree and made the pixies leap backwards with surprise. "Do you know where my baby is?"

"Oh yes, indeed we do," replied Titch.

"Sitting in our garden actually," said Mitch.

"There's a horrid witch looking for my baby," said the big tree.

"Not any more," said Mitch, puffing out his chest. "We frightened the witch away."

"Wonderful!" The big tree sounded delighted. "Will my baby be coming back?"

"Yes, just as soon as we can help it back into the woods."

So Titch and Mitch supported Little Green Tree again and walked it back to its home. In one hand Titch carried a spade to make sure that the hole that contained the roots of Little Green Tree was big enough. Once the roots were planted in the hole, they jumped up and down on the earth so that Little Green Tree would stay firmly rooted in the ground once again.